The Ride Of Our Lives

by

Alan Mason

ISBN: 9798391743668

Contents

SPRING

A SPRING REVIVAL

Life emerges from an icy grave
    scrambling to breathe again.
Clawing the ground for purchase
    despite that ache of freezing pain.
Exhaustion takes a cautious breath
    ingests the earth and the air.
The arrogant snow begins to thin
    just like an old man's hair.

Light twinkles through the prism
    rejoicing in the rainbows core.
The palette of spring conquers the bland
    punching winter on the jaw.
A knockout blow that sets the agenda
    calling out the treason.
A sleepy world rubs its eyes
    finds its focus in the season.

Stomachs swell as families grow
    furrows are scraped into the ground.
Spring sings to the naked ear
    an orchestra of life and sound.
Forgotten colours sneak into view
    a youthful beard appears on the scene.
Forests open their wardrobes
    looking for something green.

Crawling out from under winter's stone
    they pass from blindness into sight.
An excited blush of squinting red faces
    hold up hands against the light.
The newest of days born yet again
    shadows celebrate in the rising sun.
A grateful chatter worships the spring
    knowing that winter is done.

The Path

A humble path meanders through the year
    taking air and pumping blood.
It crosses the fields,
    and bridges the flood,
    it worships the flower,
    and prays for the bud.

It tip toes through the angry storm
    watches lightning crack insane.
It rumbles in the thunder,
    searches shelter from the rain,
    it feels the loss of young ones,
    and knows a parent's pain.

It's blinded by the blizzard
    and punctured by the hail.
Frozen in the midnight hours
    when strength begins to fail,
    the wind growls in defiance
    and the dark sky tells its tale.

Spring arrives and saves our lives
    as life reaches for the light.
The path breathes the deepest sigh,
    its favourite season now in sight,
    footsteps skip and thump the boards
    now free of winter's bite.

The path has lost its way
    and it lies both battered and broken.
Tumbling years have tumbled past,
    and silence is the word most spoken,
    but hope still waits for spring to fall
    and declare the winter broken.

THE PORTRAIT OF SPRING

The land has a hardened heart
    scolded by a winter's tongue.
All growth is now stunted
    cut down so very young.
A beautiful frost dresses the ground
    but hides an ugly intent.
Growth has again been spurned
    for winter pays no rent.

Suffocated by the season
    icy fingers squeeze the throat.
Choked by a frozen crust
    where noone gets to vote.
Hope scans from far away
    searching for signs of spring.
The sun breaks the horizon
    and the birds begin to sing.

A teenage beard tinged in green
    pokes through the stubborn earth.
Signalling to the underground
    that Spring is giving birth.
Colour begins to trickle
    weaving through the stubborn land.
It runs over hill and dale
    and paints the sea and sand.

The sun rides high in the midday sky
    as thoughts of winter pass away.
A warm breeze nuzzles through the trees
    and the grass kneels down to pray.
Flowers reflect the rainbows smile
    as the painters hand goes by.
A reckless love wields the brush
    as he watches the painting dry.

INNOCENCE FLAPS ITS WINGS

Lighter than the softest kiss
    and floating on the breeze.
Pretty pictures surf the warmer air
    as they peek a boo the trees.
The sun shines on stained glass wings
    a reflection of Eden's ancient light.
They gallop over flower bed fields
    and ride right out of sight.

The wing beat breaks against the air
    climbs a step on an unseen stair.
Symmetries meet without a sound
    a clap of which we are not aware.
Nectar becomes the sugary ransom
    that places the icing on the cake.
A golden jewel has life in its power
    for there is oxygen now at stake.

So be grateful for the sweet tooth
    that draws our hero to the prize.
That precious yellow powder
    worth more than all that is wise.
A tiny link in the chain of life
    ignorant of the part it plays.
Treasure each anonymous breath
    as you flutter through the day.

WAITING FOR SPRING

A forgotten light throws off its winter cloak
    for the time of hiding has now passed.
Misty daggers joust with the shadows
    piercing the darkness at last.
All time is held as the globe fails to turn
    a champion stands to claim the hour.
This dappled light brings shine and shade
    but who will gain the power ?
A picture strangely out of focus
    teased by the rays of an infant sun.
Glowering over a sad forgotten land
    lighting up the dust and the bland.
The fallen lay without remembrance
    the garlands all blown away.
Cobwebs hang loose like dirty washing
    for even the spiders didn't stay.
Stunted days stretch in expectation
    as the ball of fire struggles to rise.
Stiff muscles ache from the forced arrest
    and shadows scour the skies.
Life struggles to be born again
    seeking the sweet balm of light.
Scrubbing away at the stink of death
    blunting the teeth of winter's bite.
A new dawn cracks the sky
    breaks wide open winter's lie.
For the globe will still turn
    and the sun will still burn.
Lives will be born
    and hearts will be torn.
In an elegant cyclical truth
    where only spring holds the proof.

In The Pink

A mirror lies as still as death
    reflecting on the seasons change.
The scent of life hangs heavy on the breeze
    invading everything that breathes.
The old men of the forest
    put on their wedding suits
        to walk the aisle once more,
    scattering their confetti
        upon the woodland floor.

The bride breaks the horizon
    ancient light floods the sombre land.
No longer hidden by a murky veil
    as the darkness begins to fail.
The world is lit
    as in creations dawn
        where colour stabs the naked eye,
    shadows dance in celebration
        for they no longer have to die.

THESE HANDS

A stunned silence kidnaps the breath of creation,
    no whispering breeze,
          no rustling of the trees,
          and even the birds have no words.
The sun turns away from it's own light,
    pulling up a blanket of darkness,
          unseen tears grieve in private,
          while hope fades out of sight.

Strong hands that wrestled with chaos,
    hands that crafted the coasts,
          watered the woods,
          and even salted the sea.
Hands that threw the stars into space,
    cranked the earth for it to turn,
          and lit the sun so it could burn,
          but an apple breaks the human race.

Gentle hands embrace the kiss of iron,
    a side is split but not with laughter,
    or there would be no happy ever after,
    as heaven mourns the death of Judah's lion.
Royalty submits to stand in the gap,
    a crown of thorns to mark his reign,
    egal blood runs down the grain,
    and the cross it becomes a tree again.

INSIDE OUT

A body broken is now the only token
    that this man had taken breath.
The hope of a thousand generations
    ends in this horrific death.
Darkness falls in sorrow
    claiming the pain for its very
own.
The earth quaked for all our sake
    as it saw the empty throne.

The man is wrapped in a linen shroud
    for as he came, so he goes.
His blood stains weep for justice
    but his body feeds the crows.
Drenched now in heaven's tears
    disbelief staggers in the giddy air.
A mother's cry chokes in her chest
    as she catches a childhood stare.

A blasphemous evil grins in the
shadows
    licking his lips like a rabid beast.
Savouring every slowing heartbeat
    as the best becomes the least.
The secret of the pitch dark tomb
    where no light could appear.
Is forever held in darkness

    where even God sheds a tear.

A trumpet sounds from deep
underground
    and it's innocence that blows the
horn.
It picks the lock and turns the key
    a sacred hope has been reborn.
The ground cracks open, the spell is
broken
    the curtain hangs split and torn.
The holiest place is now in every space
    as his blood has bought the dawn.

The sun winces
    in the morning light
        the sky has never
            seemed so bright.
A vibrant hope
    clothes the land
        a future now held
            in his broken hands.

THE ANOMALY

A winged avenger rides the skies
    the crouching tiger of spring.
Flowers nod in appreciation
    As the knights take to the wing.

War paint marks the braves
    Declaring their fierce crusade.
Nectar is the sweetest heroine
    for which they buzz and crave.

Addicts on a permanent high
    instinctively seeking the prize.
Knocking at every floral door
    Hoping that the sweetness is inside.

A bumbling freak of nature
    that defies our gravities reign.
Newton turns deep in his grave
    for this striped anomaly pokes his pain.

A fluffy burglar lighter than air
    tip toes inside to steal the prize.
A sugar rush and a chemical high
    ignores those dusty yellow thighs.

But on his trousers he snags the key
    turns the ignition so we all can breathe.
In his addiction is the platform for life
    pollination,
            not just a game for the bees.

HOPE SPRINGS ETERNAL

Water runs cold and sharp
   in the night is a foe unseen.
Crystals shaken from Odin's beard
   sprinkle confetti on the scene.
Swarms of biting ice
   hunt for naked skin.
Tiny daggers thrown with skill
   to puncture and to sting.

Yuletide thoughts awaken
   strained comparisons are made.
But in this bleak midwinter deep
   hope is found in salt and spade.
These invaders from the North
   call us liars as they fall.
Conspiring in the midnight hours
   where there is no hope at all.

Welsh voices sing out proud
   but no daffodils are found.
For they lie beneath an icy shroud
   frozen deep beneath the ground.
The mad hare starts his march
   for soon he will be king.
But a blanket neatly spread
   now suffocates the spring.

Hope in perfect balance
   holds patience in her heart.
Apache drums of rhythm
   dares life to make a start.
A vampire hides in shadow
   a scent of garlic in the air.
The sun breaks through the grey
   and melts the cold away.

SPRING IN THE CITY

The sun reaches for the horizon
    causing the night to scurry away.
Leaving dark sentinels of shadow
    weaving through the early grey.

Silence tip toes through the streets
    creeps around in the darkest spaces.
Invades every mortal household
    and watches the sleeping faces.

Motionless air pretends it doesn't care
    as it's teased by the morning breeze.
A soft summer light romances the city
    and dapples through the yawning trees.

An alarm triggers this repetitive strain
    nudging at the dawn to breathe.
A car door slams and an engine fires
    and silence starts to grieve.

Furrowed brows and pounding feet
    joust amongst the pavement cracks.
Impatient glances and awkward dances
    another coffin rumbles down the track.

The jaws open as the crowds spew out
    vomited from a sweaty genetic pool.
Dirty air surrounds the travelling strangers
    and breathing in is the only fool.

Spring Takes a Bow

The curtain rises as the light takes centre stage
a hero steps into his own brilliance
but casts no shadow.

A silence dedicated to this first act
roars in the ears of all who would listen
to this orchestra of anticipation.

A tortured stillness hangs like a heavy fog
and time becomes slow and thick
balancing on the fulcrum of the season.

A dramatic intensity paints the horizon
as a fragile sky waits in the wings
nervously hoping for a leading part.

Colour interprets the rays of the sun
in a time of reflection and pride
that rebounds into a grateful sky.

The hero treads on these ancient boards
as the morning greets the dawn
and winter falls on its sword.

The Fight Back

A dirty smudge seeps into the city
    blurring the ancient lines of peace.
Drifting like a nosey neighbour
    poking in every crack and every crease.
It hangs around on street corners
    flaunting a juvenile arrogance.
Teenage smirks and leather jackets
    invite the spring to a sneaky dance.

The horizon is taken for ransom
    kidnapped by this petulant cloud.
Ghostly bonfires spread like a disease
    under this atmospheric shroud.
The seasons fight to gain dominance
    as their warriors stand face to face.
An eternal treaty has been broken
    a violation of time and space.

An icy blast from winters past
    seeks to annexe the dawning of spring.
To strangle the sun and douse the flame
    smother the songs that the birds would sing.
Daylight is compromised by shadow
    long nights whimper in the dark.
Spring stirs in a frozen captivity
    lights the fuse and releases the spark.

Winter steams as spring raises the stakes
    and temperatures wrestle in the mist.
The sun scolds winters treachery
    and by its heat the earth is kissed.
A lipstick snog that burns with lust
    that nestles in springs warm embrace.
The sky clears and daylight is king
    winter evaporates without a trace.

THE RIVER RUNS

A blue sky reflects on the lazy stream
    wondering on its journeys end.
A watery python wriggling to the sea
    seeking hope around every bend.
A gulley that courses through the land
    in nervous drought or fearful flood.
A pumping vein that rises from the earth
    bringing life and dripping blood.

Footsteps walk the wooden bridge
    creaking like an old man's knees.
Pooh sticks meander through the shadows
    twirled by the current and the breeze.
A working week melts in the rays of the sun
    as the great outside burrows deep inside.
It dries the tears of a stressful life
    as slumber yawns and enjoys the ride.

Colours explode like dynamite
    their focus as sharp as broken glass.
Boulders that feel so much older
    discover their youth in the cooling grass.
Party dress blossoms shake in anticipation
    for the time is coming to undress the trees.
A blizzard of petals swirl in the air
    the day has now caught the night's disease.

The earth turns and the sun starts to hide
    and the twilight calls as the curtain falls.
A silence grows louder than thunder
    and is heavier than castle walls.
The river continues to roll down hill
    following the secret of its anointed path.
But when breath is held and all is still
    you may even hear the river laugh.

PASSING THE BATON ON

Lanky days stride into the death of spring
    new life kisses away its youth.
Fingers are torn from the sacred rod
    as the season now learns the truth.
A repetitive cycle ordained by the gods
    where life and death share a dance.
A new season calls as the old season falls
    with no sadness or even a second glance.

The sun glares down from a blood red sky
    bringing an eerie tinge to the city.
Light comes dressed as a total stranger
    that gives no ground and spreads no pity.
The roving eye sees it all
    as it scans from the east to the west.
The season yearns as the new sun burns
    the rock turns over but will never rest.

Traffic jams make a break for the coast
    hoping for that red sky night.
Heat sizzles and spits in the burning air
    the blue sky smiles with all its might.
Summer yawns as this new day dawns
    a teary eyed spring hugs the day.
Teenage years take one last kiss
    as heavy shoulders turn away.

SUMMER

THE PROMISED LAND

Days have been wished away
 the calendar is ragged and torn.
Time has become so lazy
 as new minutes are being born.
The clock face smiles at the impatience
 as it ticks the time off our lives.
Synchronising with a beating chest
 hoping that we will survive.

Expectation measures up to reality
 excitement giggles like champagne.
Salty air fills breathless lungs
 as summer energy seems untamed.
Bare feet burrow into velvet sand
 and waves wash the pilgrim's feet.
Licking them with a seaside breeze
 strangling the seasons heat.

Thunder grumbles in the churning waves
 squeals of laughter run the lanes.
White horses gallop to beat the tide
 catching rainbows in their manes.
Sandwiches made with real sand
 give a crunch to the egg and cress.
Sloppy cones that drip on sandy phones
 and the gulls gorge on what is left

A bonfire burns on the horizon
 bleeding through the summer sky.
An embarrassed sun turns away
 hoping it will rise another day.
Footprints drown in the incoming tide
 an off shore wind kicks over the traces.
Eradicating any signs of life
 a new day may never see their faces.

The Star In The East

The water ripples like dark chocolate
    a slow rhythmic tap slaps the bow.
Stillness holds hands with the silence
    nothing stirs and there's no other sound.

The morning stretches and yawns at the dawn
    knuckles burrow into sleepy eyes.
Creeping shadows begin to dance in the light
    as they feel the temperature rise.

The star in the east throws off its cloak
    turns the night into borrowed rags.
A tramp that owns the midnight hours
    with a rusty trolley and dirty bags.

A rite of passage glows in the misty air
    a line drawn on the chocolate sea.
A bearing pointing to the newest of days
    where the air we breathe
        will always be free.

The sun winks at humanity
    and beams the warmest smile.
Strong forces rotate the floating rocks
    so we all get the heat at least for a while.

In the darkness, the light still falls
    on the small boats
        and the chocolate lakes.
For light and shadow
    are bound to one another
        for as one sleeps
            the other wakes.

The Pretty Maids

A quiet humility stands to attention
    out of the reach of the stretching tide.
A sandy blizzard blows through the ranks
    while new paint hides the pain inside.
A forgotten time struggles to remember
    when Victoria blessed these summer lands.
A time when bare skin was hidden as a sin
    a daring criminal that now stalks the sands.

Tears cascade down the forgotten years
    and footsteps no longer tread the boards.
Package holidays are being unwrapped
    the local economy falls on its sword.
So the locals wake up and put on their make up
    smile the smiles of a defeated foe.
For plastic cash can't buy the weather
    or bring warmth to an icy blow.

The pretty maids mourn the passing season
    as the autumn leaves begin to turn.
No footprints walk in this desolate sand
    and the barbecues no longer burn.
A silence shouts with all its might
    and even the waves forget to roar.
The beach has become a sandy morgue
    life now lies in an icy drawer.

But the earth will turn and the sun will rise
    and tomorrow will become today.
A plot of many twists and turns
    which the pretty maids will dance away.
They stare out to the shore line
    listening to the music of the beach.
A rhythmic wake of drag and break
    that will always be just out of reach.

Castles In The Sand

They say a picture paints a thousand words
    but so many more are left unsaid.
Our minds grope around in the darkness
    but it's a light that has already fled.
Do we dare to decode the brush strokes
    as they interpret our darkest fears.
Indelible scars that gather strength
    as regret wrings out the tears.
The castle once stood out bold and strong
    as it shook the hand of the rising sun.
Banners furling on the easterly breeze
    bells chiming that the day has begun.
The hustle and bustle of happy lives
    chatter and banter duck and dive.
They dance on the green in the fading light
    where old age sneers at the pretty sight.
Time now tightly holds the reins
    and it can check you in or check you out.
Arrogance skates on the thinnest of ice
    a mask that hides a worrying doubt.
Simple tasks become as hard as iron
    thoughts struggle to contact the mouth.
Backs break and hands begin to shake
    and all that was tight has now gone
                  south.
The ramparts lose the battle with time
    and the flags lay limp and torn.
The mighty granite has crumbled
    no bells ring at the break of the dawn.
Nothing in the moat will now ever float
    wrecks lie abandoned in the shallows.
Dark hulks that no longer sail for battle
    while victory swings alone in the gallows.
So we build our castles in the sand
    believing they will stand and never fall.
A dream that drowns in each incoming tide
    a persistent force that will break any wall.
So as you watch from your ivory tower
    convinced that you do have the power.
But as the wind blows and the waves break
    to believe you are king is a deadly mistake.

A Chink Of Light

The day begins to turn its back
    as a lazy sun sinks into the west.
Sadness sighs in the failing light
    as the horizon slips into the night.
The sky picks at the oldest of wounds
    as the darkness strangles another day.
The daylight kneels and prays for the dawn
    a time when vows
                and promises are sworn.

Friends look back to a different day
    where laughter and memories collide.
Emotions seep through their stories
    as pain and regret come in on the tide.
A grown up stranger that looks familiar
    stares back at me in black and white.
Blood runs into the sunset
    as the twilight starts to bite.

Silence whispers quietly
    into the ear of no return.
No breath of air blows anywhere
    as the skyline begins to burn.
The crows don't crow and the trees don't creak
    nothing moves and noone speaks.
The day begins to cough and choke
    as the dusk throws down its heavy cloak.

Four decades have now run under the bridge
    enough water to drown a million seas.
But teenage years still bathe in golden tears
    a time when we thought we had the keys.
We smile a smile of recognition
    as we toast the last rays of the failing sun.
And so we watch the day just fade away
    as hope stares down the barrel of a gun.

WHO SAYS BUCKETS DON'T CRY?

A ragged surf drags itself up the beach
    clawing talons scoring the soggy ground.
The sand glistens as the ocean breathes in
    and then spits out a thundering sound.
Footprints made by passing strangers
    wiped clean like chalk on a board.
Names left for the sky to treasure
    for the tide drowns both the rich and poor.

I remember those days we spent in June
    when we danced to the summers tune.
We made paper boats that struggled to float
    around castles that had broken moats.
We built dams across sandy streams
    searched for shells and ice cream dreams.
We were held in the arms of a benevolent sun
    unaware that the winter would come.

The days got up late
    and the morning stretched
    the afternoon yawned and slept instead.
    the evenings were short
    the sun coffined with the dead.

The beach was empty
    even the seaweed stayed away.
The tide did its usual thing
    just in and out around the bay.
But they left us behind
    they didn't care and didn't mind.
We still remember the days we played
    hope you are well
            from the Bucket and Spade.

JUST EMPTY SHELLS

I walked through a seaside graveyard
where so many had lived and died.
Their bones cracked beneath my feet
washed away by an innocent tide.
Black suits stand wearing sombre faces
had any tears even cried ?
A minute's silence to appease our guilt
was it war or was it suicide ?

Infinity defined by empty shells on a beach
a countless mountain that noone could reach.
They've been soaked and choked
prodded and poked
loved for a day and then thrown away.
The pretty ones seem to do okay
as their bones shine like precious stones
blessed by that light in the sky.

As we squeeze ourselves into smaller spaces
we bump into neighbouring lives.
Boundaries become a hostile barrier
and "Good Morning" becomes a lie.
Every day resembles all the other days
and routine rules the roost.
The expectation is suffocation
freedom just won't shake loose.

So we become just like empty shells
waiting for the tide to have its day.
Politely isolating
pretending that we're renovating.
Our lives become so small
and some even nothing at all.
So we wait upon the beach
hoping that we aren't out of reach.

A Blast From The Past

Tears run down wrinkled cheeks
    a distant memory has detonated the day.
Aching sobs gulp like a fish out of water
    as an unexpected stranger has come to stay.
A forgotten moment swallows the present
    under a royal blue sky and a burning sun.
The ocean waved as though it knew my name
    and the waves hit the nails in one by one.

This little girl I had forgotten
    running and jumping before my very eyes.
Giggles and laughter danced together
    when did I bid these moments goodbye.
A curious warmth flowed from the picture
    it began to comfort my beating heart.
But the fleeting time of so many years
    was still able to break my heart apart.

The years had turned into decades
    and so much had been left behind.
A tension grew as those tiny dreams
    came in and out with the flowing tide.
It was a time when unicorns were real
    and dragons flew across the sky.
Solutions were found in a plaster and a kiss
    we didn't know that family would die.

A beautiful time of innocence
    that becomes more guilty every day.

OUT FOR LUNCH

Thoughts of work are shed like dirty clothes
    as a heavy week is put to bed.
Thoughts fight and jostle for priority
    decisions still weigh as heavy as lead.
Footsteps pound as they barely touch the ground
    but escape is a filthy liar.
The car doors slam as the engine fires
    beeping horns and squealing tyres.

Under the boughs of the dappling trees
    the sun finds a way to pierce the shade.
Tension and worry slowly drift away
    as laughter ripples through the glade.
Like a snake as it sheds its skin
    the stress of work slides in the bin.
As the heart slows and normality grows
    it's easier now to let the breath in.

Familiar voices shout my name
    excited that I've made it this time.
They run and grab my legs
    and the day begins to rhyme.
Cheese and onion, scotch eggs
    smokey bacon and chicken legs.
A wine that flows from the heart of France
    another day, another chance.

We play and doze on the chequered cloth
    soaking in the warmth of summer.
We hug and giggle, tickle and wriggle
    but still we must pay the drummer.

For stress dangles at the end of a rope,
    a crouching tiger,
            on a slippery slope.

THE SPOTLIGHT

I am the ground, I am the soil
I am the fossil, I am the oil.
    I am the seed, I am the grain
    I am the sun, I am the rain.
I am all that grows
    for I am the nettle
        and I am the rose.
I am the blood, I am the beat
I am the trick, I am the treat.
    I am the breath, I am the brain
    I am the senile, I am the sane.
I am all that breathes ………
    for I am the man
        and I am the trees.
I am the sprint, I am the jog
I am the focus, I am the fog.
    I am the stealth, I am the sting
    I am the boxer, I am the ring.
I am the passing time ……………..
    for I am the moment
        and I am the chime.

I am the riches, I am the rags
I am the edges, I am the snags.
    I am the triumph, I am the trial
    I am an inch, I am a mile.
I am every choice…………
    for I am the thought
        and I am the voice.
I am the silence, I am the sound
I am the hidden, I am the found.
    I am the vision, I am the call
    I am the rise, I am the fall.
I am every part……………..
    for I am the beat
        and I am the heart,
for I am the spotlight and I see it all.

It's Only Your Perspective

Light dives through the window
a heroic attempt to save the day.
An old time movie flickers
but there's nothing on the screen today.
A recurring theme of black and white
as the champions wrestle the throne.
These caped crusaders need no mask
for it's their shadows that are thrown.

They patiently wait for the cycle to turn
they know that one will fall and burn.
A cosmic pattern that controls the tides
that turns the spinster into a bride.
The veil is hers during the daylight hours
but the dark creeps up the daylight towers.
Shadows that are born in the brightest light
believe they have the numbers to fight.

But the corridor sees the truth and the lies
for it houses the obvious and the surprise.
For shadows fall and light fails
and mistrust lies deep within the rails.
A promise dangles and teases the road
enticing a hope that will never erode.
A vanishing point that won't disappear
the longest road just eats up the years.

It's an infinite chase
    a never ending race,
      to an unreachable place,
          that disappears without trace.

At The End Of The Pier

He hangs his head at the end of the pier
    sensing that the Almighty is here.
The tiniest part of the landscape
    filled with wonder and fear.
The snow caped mountains still run red
    as they wait the roll of the dice.
Reflection and recollection
    recognise an unpayable price.
For the anger in the sky never sleeps
    and the turmoil festers in the deep.

Contemplation drags a heavy weight
    scoring a scar across a broken deal.
Robes of purple garnish a sea of tears
    and guilt writhes like a slippery eel.
Regret stirs the stagnant pool
    with a bright new shiny blade.
Innocence splashes at the water's edge
    unaware and unafraid.
For it was for just this moment
    that the cross of wood was made.

A place for the guilt to hang
    in a noose that's already tied.
At the foot there is the chance to kneel
    to shed those tears you've never cried.
Heavy boulders that lay on tired shoulders
    quarried by darkness and fear.
Self doubt begins to shout
    as a slimy voice creeps out.
It says the young man is not so strong
    but now is the time to sing his song.

LIVING ON THE EDGE

Communities cling together
    their backs hard against the wall.
Painted lives on a concrete cliff
    where even eagles fear the fall.
Houses are thrown like clumsy dice
    while the wheel in the casino spins.
A cheeky gamble that comes up trumps
    for the house is rigged to win.

A town held in granite arms
    where danger walks among the charms.
Fault lines falter and crevices crack
    it seems the mountain is fighting back.
Little by little and day by day
    safety is falling into the bay.
A hungry tide swallows the shore
    as hope prays for one more day.

Generations have gone about their little lives
    but beauty has now become the beast.
Tourism lurks round every corner
    and walks down every street.
Red faces sweat in their holiday shirts
    and tanned legs wear their tiny skirts.
Their cameras capture grateful faces
    but inside there are painful spaces.

Gratitude has now become an attitude
    as the autumn leaves begin to turn.
For tourist dollars have paid the ransom
    as this Italian summer burns.
This maybe a pearl of great price
    but this rock has also become a home.
Where people live and ride the tide
    two hundred miles from Rome.

SAND FLIES

They arrive like a biblical plague
    swarming the sand and shore.
Escaping from tedious lives
    excited for what's in store.
They cram the car parks
    and traffic jam the roads.
They jump the pavements
    and break every code.
Lines have been drawn,
    and oaths have been sworn.
Pale skins bake
    as claims are staked.
The umbrella goes up but it ain't gonna rain
for its shade that is needed to ride this train.
Sandwiches adopt a crunchy bite
and ice cream cones melt out of sight.

The sun sets and the light begins to fail
    and light bulbs challenge the fading glow.
A soft breeze fills the snow white sails
    and a stillness waits for the night to show.
Bins gorge on the holiday trash
    and then puke at the end of the day.
Spilling their guts in the failing light
    while the gulls eat but never pay.
The day ends with the sounds of the sea
    drowning all that is left of the beach.
A rhythm that invites a waking sleep
    to a place that we can never reach.
But tomorrow is still within our grasp
even though we sleep the midnight hours.
The morning breaks and the day awakes
and declares this day is ours.

THE DAY SUMMER DIED

In this amphitheatre of seaside dreams
    sand and salt water dance on the tide.
Indelible memories engraved on the heart
    lingering images of a time that's died.
Sandcastle making and tent peg staking
    fancy flip flops and posh fish and chips.
The thunderous smack of waves against rock
    and the softest brush of teenage lips.

Bouncy castles wobble like a night out
    children search for rock pool treasure.
And laughter chases the reluctant sea
    while champagne surf toasts the shore.
Schools of dolphins and crazy golfing
    silhouette sunsets slide into the west.
Evening clouds mirror rosy cheeks
    proclaiming the day is blessed.

Vacancies swing on rusted chains
    filthy curtains mourn the breeze.
Grimy windows hide an inner turmoil
    a local economy on bended knees.
Holiday pennies now spent far away
    on an all-inclusive sunshine bake.
Past footsteps walk the empty sand
    while seaweed drifts on a salty wake.

Dark clouds gather, blotting out the light
    hungry to snuff out the eastern flame.
Ghostly fingers reach to pinch the air
    stifling the seabirds cry of blame.
The seaside pulses with a gritty malice
    veins throb on shattered brows.
A quiet stillness implies a coming storm
    and a loud silence takes a bow.

AUTUMN

WHAT GOES AROUND COMES AROUND

A stranger dares to challenge the sun
    turning his back on the javelins of light.
Spears thrown in defiance and fear
    as the bark of Autumn comes to bite.
The shadow smiles behind a faceless mask
    chuckles are heard in the rustling leaves.
Temperature falls on the sword of the season
    and even colour begins to grieve.

Knuckles on naked twiggy fingers crack
    as the blast from the North rattles the trees.
A cowering landscape holds back the tears
    as decay crunches and swirls in the breeze.
The moody sky gives voice to a breaking heart
    a rib cage shattered in torment.
A dark cloak falls and snuffs out the light
    an unwelcome tenant that pays no rent.

Rivers surround and swallow the ancient stones
    as the sodden hills flush their chains.
Excited currents jockey for position
    but its gravity that rides this train.
A pinball game without control
    banks are broken and burst.
The impatient tide paces back and forth
    desperate to drown its growing thirst

The thrones of many seasons past lay empty
    dungeons filled with chains and despair.
An ancient wheel creaks as time begins to turn
    the hands stir and a pulse beats the air.
The deep underground stretches and yawns
    unaware that there is change in sight.
Hope seeps into tired and hidden spaces
    and darkness cowers
                from the morning light.

As Time Passes By

Humanity trundles by living only in that moment
      breathing and grieving
          hoping and scoping.
Lives as different as the east is from the west,
      all mining the same narrow gully,
          hoping for gold in the dirt.
Broken hearts break again, punching the lip of love
      needing and bleeding,
          sighing and crying.
Tears dribble into salty puddles of emotion,
    smiles imprisoned behind gritted teeth,
      a snotty paste sticks on the smile.

Sooner or later they arrive at platform nowhere
    roasted and toasted,
        lost and tossed.
Comfort is found cradled on an empty bench,
    where initials were carved by desperate hands,
      shouting "I know where you are"

Countless footsteps have echoed through the years
    walking and talking,
      jogging and slogging.
Strides that reach for the future or long for the past,
    each contact marking the passing of time,
      a time when someone was there.

WE ALL FALL DOWN

A tired sun drops below the horizon,
realising defeat as the seasons fight.
The light fades into darkness and dusk,
autumn ascends the throne by right.
Death strides into a growing reality,
green takes on an earthy brown.
Mr Farenheit reluctantly drops to his knees,
and summer concedes the crown.

Butterflies of hope flutter in the breeze,
searching for life in the shade of the trees.
But the canopy is lost as the leaves are shed,
a crunchy carpet now woven with the dead.
The bones of summer linger on the ground,
but soon the blanket will have no sound.
In to the earth the season will fade,
ruthlessly slaughtered by winter's blade.

A never ending dance of ebb and flow,
a polite veneer masking a deadly intent.
A snarl that hides behind a sickly smile,
where what is said, is not what is meant.
So the game is played, the dice are thrown,
but the outcome is already known.
For the autumn leaves know when to fall
and the summer sun shines on us all.

So we circle round as children do
we also ring a ring a rose or two
pockets full of smiles or frowns
 and then of course we all fall down.

The Snuffler

Summer's death carpets the woodland floor
where fallen leaves and broken hearts
    search for love no more.
Autumn's whisper stirs the unclothed trees
red faced branches struggle
    to hide their dignity.
But in the midst of despair hope lingers
    there for teeny tiny footsteps
      tip toe everywhere.
He scurries along through the secret paths
    a compass now written on his soul
    taught upon the knee and hearth.
A surface mole that digs through leaves
    camouflaged by natures touch
    and noone hears him breathe.

A bandit of the forest wears his mask with pride
    he snuffles in the undergrowth
    and shovels dirt aside.
A mobile pin cushion that shouts beware
    a curled up spikey fortress
    marked "handle this with care".
The solstice drives a changing dawn
    as autumn bows to winter's crown
    and the snuffler begins to yawn.
The paths lay empty as the temperature falls
    no snuffling can be seen or heard
    but underground his bedtime calls.

It's Just That Time Of Year

Sadness runs as thick as treacle
    clogging that chance to smile.
Rain falls from the darkest skies
    and tears fall from the saddest eyes.
Bringing to mind all that is not said
    reflecting that this summer is dead.
Short days long for the right to stay
    as dusk kidnaps the day away.
The village clock chimes the count of five
    as a new darkness comes alive.
Romantic embers dance in the heat
    as they smoulder at the dusky street.
Shining through a tear stained glance
    dreaming of just one more chance.
Tree confetti blows away
    for they'll be no wedding here today.
A lonely bench dreams of better times
when it welcomed those evening chimes.
The sunshine charges the balmy air
    strangers would sit without a care.
Grateful for the dappled shade
    as the leaves in the sunlight played.
The crickets sang their scratchy tune
    and the sun reached out to turn on the moon.

The trams chatter down the rails
    in a language noone knows.
The outside takes a seat inside
    swaying on this clattering ride.
A rented space on a very short lease
    where a palm must be greased.
Jostled together in a genetic store
    with drunken staggers to the door.
From a distance a restless winter watches
    eager for the baton to be passed.
In the park the rusty swings are still
    and the slides no longer slide.
An icy breath blows through the town
    blood freezing in its veins.
A low chuckle runs down the alleyways
    and dances through the lanes.

Heaven's Gate

Life can turn in a moment
    as it slithers around our dreams.
A giant snake navigating our decisions
    a mystery gnawing at the seams.
Potential shouts at all who travel
    you are the king, you are the day.
Reality surfs a more dangerous tide
    not black or white just murky grey.

Certainty is an elusive stranger
    as probability rocks the boat.
Playing the odds can be dangerous
    they can grab you by the throat.
Tip toe through the time bombs
    slowly sneak under the wire.
Freedom is an imaginary beast
    flying high and breathing fire.

I wake myself but in a dream
    an autumn lane beneath my feet.
The shimmer of the golden leaves
    draw my eyes to a golden seat.
Where a carpet of a million lives
    pave the way on which I tread.
The light of a thousand summers
    connecting the living to the dead.

The threshold lies before me
    one more step and I am lost.
Like stepping on the pavement cracks
    there must always be a cost.
But it isn't scorching burning fire
    but brilliant shining light.
I look around and I'm not alone
    as we kneel before the throne.

THE SEASONS OF OUR LIVES

In the Summer of '75 …………..
everything was enough
no routines or lists of stuff.
The only commitment was getting up
and sometimes we didn't even do that.
We built dens in the woods
and climbed the trees if we could.
We swam in the open sea
and climbed the headland rocks.
Barbecues burning on the beach
our parents far from reach.
We smoked in the bus shelters
bought pasties from the pub.
We were the greatest players of the day
kicking a ball into the early grey.
When the street lights went on
we still carried on.
We threw up on strong cider
and choked on strong cigars.
We dreamed of love
and the fastest cars.
But when Elvis died
even strong men cried.

It was Queen who now topped the charts
their lyrics even now burst our hearts.
Bohemian Rhapsody
"Mama just killed a man…………."
And we wasted days just being friends
believing that they would never end.

In the Autumn of '20 ……….
We still know our names
but we are different and the same.
Our parents lie deep underground
legends of our childhood past.
In a tiny village long ago
where did all those decades go ?
Mistakes and poor decisions
punctuate the time.
Regret has many stories to tell
as so many dreams died as well.
Children ease the pain
as we live our lives again.
As I look I can almost see it all
as I watch the leaves of autumn fall.

YOU'VE GOT TO BE JOKING

The dusk has fallen early
    tripping over   late October.
Dark stories will be told
    eerie sounds will fill the night.
Creaking doors and midnight cries
    of beasts that growl and bite.

Nervous laughter breaks
    as they wait at the garden gate.
Fangs, fear and fake blood
    flow as they go and trick or treat.
Tears trickle but not in sorrow
    as giggles run down the street.

Knock Knock
    the key is scraping in the lock.
The door swings and the hinges sing
    the light blinds their childish sight.
A dark shadow ten feet tall
    climbs up and over the garden wall.

A ghostly robe stumbles
    and tumbles through the weeds.
Death by a thousand cuts
    as the thorns and brambles bite.
A high pitched wail pierces the air
    as the ghostly ghoul falls out of sight.

A deep voice bellows and cries
    "Risk Assessment please,
    Yep you in the sheet behind the trees.
    That's a trip hazard not a scary disguise.
    and I hope those eyes
                are regulation size.
A naked flame, you're off your head
    that's how people end up dead.
Your costumes not fireproof
        you'll end up as toast."
"Unless I really am a GHOST ...."

ALL HALLOWS EVE

A celebration of darkness
　　as autumn falls into shadow.
Colours seep slowly away
　　ignored and unwanted.
We pull up the collar of our lives
　　fastened with fingers crossed.
Short days wrestle with long nights
　　held in a hold they cannot break.

A fight begins as the Earth turns
　　signalling a recurring nightmare.
The horizon cannot bear to look
　　as it peeps through childish fingers.
The pagans bob their apples
　　and dance round ancient trees.
The righteous fill their chapels
　　spend the night on bended knees.

A nasty rattling laugh chuckles
　　rising from the depths of the past.
Broken teeth show the scars of defeat
　　gummy lips flap but make no sound.
Smoke rises from the bonfire of tradition
　　as religion strikes the match.
Kidnapping this day for their own
　　the battle won without a scratch.

A day to remember or a night to forget
　　as differing cultures come face to face.
They look each other right in the eye
　　reflecting the face they think they know.
What we see in the face of another
　　is our own snarling desire to be right.
A diminishing image of common ground
　　although shadows do form in the light.

THE MAN WHO LIT THE MATCH

A secret lurks deep underground
    the stench of conspiracy fills the air.
The London fog provides the cover
    to hide the dragon in his lair.

A nettle grows in the religious earth
    watered by discord and power.
Secret talks in the dead of night
    as treason starts to flower.

Treachery treads a dangerous path
    and the gallows smirk in hope.
For truth is unstable and trust is a lie
    and guilty necks will feel the rope.

Democracy hangs by an unlit fuse
    just waiting for the kiss of flame.
A hand trembles to engage the strike
    will he suffer shame or fame.

Down in the catacombs
    where the rats live in shadow.
A naked flame, a time for decision
    the gunpowder plot is about to blow.

Four hundred years later
    we're still planting plots.
Not with powder but clever words
    for the fight for power never rots.

So we build the bonfires
    and we burn the guy.
An ancient rebellion fails
    as the flames begin to die.

We smell the smoke
    and we're drawn to the embers.
Mesmerised in the moment
    and still we remember.

MIND GAMES

A bronze statue forged in flame
    caught in a moment of time.
Everything is still, nothing moves
    a stationary revelation.
A burning portrait that has much to tell
    a story that lies within a story.
As memory grinds through the slides
    searching for recognition.

But the harder you look the more you see
    as the mind fights for clarity.
Fear begins to stalk this unknown land
    as level ground begins to slide.
The concrete of a 2 dimensional space
    now swings nervously in the balance.
A layer of perceptive interpretation
    wraps the suffocating landscape.

Do you dare to stare into the fire
    as the mind plays its games.
A sense of seeing but not seeing
    in a mesmerising unreality.
The image becomes the focus
    as light bounces off the page.
Creatures morph in the breathing flame
    no longer captured in the frame.

What does the eye of the mind perceive
    as the flames flicker and weave.
They lick at the edges of imagination
    stretching the sinew to tension.
Inviting courage for a second glance.
    as hope and fear swirl in the dance.
A mind tattooed by an invisible hand
    hoping that the ashes
                won't make a stand.

THE FUTURE CALLS

What thoughts ride the wild wind
    in this turmoil of doubt and decision.
Stick or twist the hand must be played
    but will it bring truth or will it bring treason.
Damned if I do and damned if I don't
    pros and cons openly lie to my face.
A tightrope strung over a deep canyon
    dangerously lost without a trace.

Memories tweak the nose of truth
    as they hide in sentimental shadows.
Chaotically woven between fact and fiction
    a middle ground where nothing grows.
A hopeful stare gazes into a future time
    a lighthouse desperately seeking clarity.
Cutting through the foggy path of stalemate
    clearing the brambles of regret and pity.

Sparks fly to demand my attention
    squinting retinas frown in the fizzing light.
Vision stands mesmerised by fleeting lives
    drawn to the simplicity flashing in the night.
Forever is long but the days are short
    many of them over before they've begun.
The spark of life stunted by to and fro'
    where torment shortens the days in the sun.

THE CONTRAST

Seasonal colours catch the light of the moon
    drawing eyes to the shade of decay.
Leafy butterflies dance without a care
    stealing the spotlight of the suns last ray.

But soon they will fall despite this moment
    their grip broken a finger at a time.
Ground into the midnight dirt
    trodden and sodden is the crime.

The wick of the candle is snuffed
    but in the dirt a miracle thrives.
Lost in the quicksand of the woodland floor
    a spark of life strives to survive.

A remnant works through the palette
    searching for its Sunday best.
The easel is set as the colours flow
    will the brush strokes face the test.

Life senses the changing light
    a jump start that shakes the ground.
The magician switches red to green
    they leave the grid without a sound.

On the journey of a recurring nightmare
    a carousel ride to genocide.
Roots and shoots tip toe through the maze
    gently pushing death aside.

A heartbeat now brings a rhythm
    the steady pulse of an ancient drum.
Calling the troops out of the trenches
    but in this season
        will they still come ?

The Angry Sky

An angry sky scoffs at the failing sun
    a rumble filled with "I told you so".
Darkness hovers in the distance
    still wary of the amber glow.
The equinox jogs its steady course
    another stagnant mooch into gloom.
Time is crunched between the craggy cogs
    squeezed into this seasonal tomb.

The day shrinks as the night explodes
    light sulks as its brilliance wains.
Vision scrambles for fire and flame
    in the twilight where the shadows reign.
The wind whispers to the gathering cloud
    promising treasure in the golden land.
A ravenous winter gorges on the timid days
    the colours of autumn painted bland.

WINTER

Early December

Snow arrogantly falls without apology
    claw marks rake the street
        as rubber hunts for safe passage.
Lines of coke snorted by passing traffic
    snuffling up the wicked dust
        as fake garlands swing in innocence.

Pedestrians mooch in frustration
    so many doors, so many floors.
        the penalty for hunting treasure.
Overdrawn into a fragile shiny reality
    where twinkly lights itch for the switch
        and ancient rhymes dance in the air.

Empty wallets and broken hearts
    console each other as the calendar turns
    and flames ignite as the bank balance burns.
More breeds more as we search every store
    a hopeful request for bigger and better
        as we must fulfil the old guys letter.

A shackled expectation reaches for the moon
    where guilt battles with an honest reality
        born out of want rather than need.
Imported crap wrapped in a seasonal cloak
    shop windows sneer as the cash flow chokes
        the rent is spent and the plastic bleeds.

METAMORPHOSIS

The forest has been stripped
    of its coat of many colours
        as autumn bleeds into the earth.
Naked branches blush
    as blood red blossom
        deny the grey of winter's birth.

Tangled and tortured in confusion
    a rattling joust of branch and brier
        where weeping bark breaks no stone.
A skeletal x-ray of a fading landscape
    a ghostly creaking stalks the woods
        while whispering leaves sleep alone.

A freezing breath blows through the land
    as a sleepy sun struggles to rise
        a friendly wink in a heavy sky.
Frosty jackets bring no warmth
    deadly cocoons that slow the beat
        how we long for the butterfly.

OUT OF THE SHADOW

Moss covered stones lay broken
    written by a lightning hand.
A shining face now grows dim
    as holy granite turns to sand.
The angel has passed over
    precious blood stains the doors.
The desert claims a generation
    while in the distance a lion roars.

A light shines in the darkness
    as a daring hope takes centre stage.
Life and death kneel on softer ground
    as opportunity turns the page.
Old is new and new is old
    as boundaries lose their power.
A promise blooms in the darkest of rooms
    this is the day, the time, the hour.

A baby cries in the dead of night
    a lament for the heart of man.
A scream that scrambles the wise
    like broken eggs in a greasy pan.
Fear crawls up the establishment walls
    as ancient texts creep up the spine.
Pennies drop and even boulders fall
    as wide eyed realisation walks the line.

A stable models this ironic scene
    no gilded throne for the infant king.
The trumpets lay silent, no banquet is laid
    there's no royal seal or diamond ring.
A blood soaked rag is all that is worn
    apart from a crown that is made of thorns.
A dawn like no other breaks this day
    for a new humanity now walks this way.

The Gift

The sculptor senses a potential in the ice
    as it calls from the stubborn block.
A telepathic reach for freedom
    cries out from the frozen rock.

He listens with a sculptor's ear
    to the voice of shape and form.
Interpreting the muffled sounds
    so the sculpture can be born.

A welcome pain begins to ache
    the ransom for his skill and sight.
A misty dream of shifting shadows
    boldly swaggers into the light.

Shade and texture find their calling
    as edges appear and definition grows.
He walks around the image in his mind
    and then the chisel starts the show.

Features come out of hiding
    as temperatures rise in the core.
Time is quickly chipping away
    as water pools upon the floor.

THE GATHERING

Humanity swarms as the globe spins
    the galaxies smile
        as they watch the migration.
Scurrying and hurrying to catch the dream
    walking and stalking
        as they fall into temptation.

They worship at a tree that never dies
    no autumn leaves
        or twig like frames.
Stars twinkle in the evergreen boughs
    seeping and peeping
        like flickering flame.

Piles of hidden wishes wait in darkness
    delicately holding
        a silent breath.
The fizz of champagne breaks over the bow
    sipping and dripping
        as secrets find their death.

A CHRISTMAS PRESENT

A stowaway stirs in the starlit eaves,
as the icy breath of winter weaves,
    a spell that brings a crystal sheen
    and footsteps stay where feet have been.
Hidden treasures beat their chest
    as they wake from their seasons rest.

Hallowed crates descend from on high
reminders of how the years go by
    a dancing Santa and a shiny star
    a reindeer that plays a broken guitar.
Childhood stockings dangle in hope
    while laughter groans at the same old jokes.

The scissors and the sellotape decide to elope
and the cards of Christmas just sit and gloat
    the twinkly lights refuse to shine
    bulbs leapfrog up the line.
Manic children just won't be told
    and the Parson's Nose has caught a cold.

The secret recipes can't be found
ancient rites to which we're bound
    name tags hang from tinsel boughs
    memorials in the here and now.
The turkey slips and makes a dive
    but he won't get out of here alive.

THE CABIN

An enduring sadness lurks in the glade
    as it skulks amongst the trees.
An unseen smoke that peeps round corners
    and dodges past the breeze.
It crawls through open windows,
    and it sneaks under the door.
It lives in the ageing cracks,
    and breeds under the floor.

The cabin echoes with footsteps of the past
    family sounds engrained in ancient walls.
Laughter lies deep in the plaster
    and life echoes down the halls.
Happy tears have wept
    for the times when children played
But in all the generations past
    they always seem to run away.

A garden grown for sunshine
    has now fallen into shadow.
Barbed wire briars poke and choke
    in a place where nothing grows.
Granite stones stand in line
    like strong soldiers on parade.
Watching over the sleeping forms
    where the families have been laid.

The seasons bring no comfort
    as darkness hides behind the glass.
As still as death the cabin waits
    for another century to pass.
Giggles run down the twisting path
    children's chatter disturbs the day.
The front door creaks and opens wide
    for another family to step inside.

For Whom The Bell Tolls

An eerie silence waits for death
　　as the minutes march the trail.
Tiny strides take up the beat
　　as midnight takes a breath.

The sky explodes as the hands coincide
　　spears of light puncture the darkness.
Smoke lays thick like a pea soup fog
　　strangers hug and hearts collide.

The passing year is turned away
　　thrown on a heap of bygone years.
A card that once had known his name
　　now flutters in the city's breeze.

The old fades away as the new catches fire
　　the skyline pulses with a heavy beat.
They know they are different but also the same
　　brothers just passing through a delicate time.

The New Year bathes in adoration
　　as the crowds revel in its touch.
A fresh start beats in many chests
　　but optimism drowns in shallow booze.

The night grows dark as the javelins fall
　　a sudden silence that triggers reality.
The dark hours pass like a dripping tap
　　heavy hangovers wince in the light.

The dawn breaks and smashes the mood
　　headlines shout as the revellers sleep.
A new broom sweeps the past away
　　under the carpet it's the only way.

The Heart Of The Matter

I declared my love that day
    as we walked through the shallow wood.
Not out loud but deep inside
    where love still wore a hood.
Cowering in a teenage heart
    worshipping where she stood.

A delicious pain danced with torture
    dosey doeing out of step and out of time.
Filled with an awkward innocence
    where nothing seems to rhyme.
Aching hours of anticipation
    where even seconds are a crime.

We carved our symbol in a tree
    a heart cut deep inside the grain.
An ironic act of a child's first love
    daubed by this treacherous stain.
The bark cries out for retribution
    as the tree endures my pain.

THE EYE

A lidless eye that never sleeps
    a laser slicing through our conscience.
Skewering that wriggling guilt
    like a worm on a hook.

Light is sucked into the iris
    where it deciphers the human code.
Chewed on, tasted and spat out
    a bland flavourless phlegm.

It sees the hiding and hears the lies
    knows the pretending and defending.
The endless thrust and parry
    of being more than we are.

It monitors the lines of every life
    as humanity draws a hopeful future.
Careful sketches and violent scribbles
    squabble as silent dreams collide.

A tear freezes on winter's cheek
    beckoned by an arrogant nonsense.
For everything leads to the crossroads
    where all our choices must be weighed.

THE WINTER SOLSTICE

The priests bend the knee in the failing light
    an eerie heavy silence hangs in the air.
The earth quakes
    and the sky breaks
    as darkness crawls from its summer lair.

Brooding temples wait in anticipation
    the eclipse of the season smothers the dawn.
The daylight shrinks
    as the ball of light sinks
    and the winter solstice is reborn.

Ancient stones hum a low inaudible tone
    the wind is held and the air as still as death.
The whole planet grieves
    as the silent dawn weaves
    a spell that steals away our breath.

The Earth revolves through the darkness
    as a desperate light chases the shadow.
A race that must be won
    to regain the light of the sun
    as we wait for the rise of tomorrow.

In Every Life A Little
Rain Must Fall

Sadness falls in little pieces
    sobbing into a pool of sorrow.
Hearts wade deeper into despair
    aching to reach tomorrow.
The wrinkled surface mirrors
    an ageing forlorn brow.
Ripples reach out for the comfort
    that reality does not allow.

Emptiness grinds its ugly teeth
    gnawing on fragile plans.
Familiar has become a stranger
    as they reach to take my hand.
Guilty platitudes take the stage
    as the snakes taste the air.
Flappy lips form unheard words
    and I just pretend to care.

The alarm goes off
    but the day never dawns.
The duvet snuggles me away
    holds me in the warm.
Everything seems inside out
    hope rides the darkest horse.
Taste has gone and eaten itself
    and flavour needs much more sauce.

Colour drains from ruddy faces
    ghosts grin in black and white.
Tears paint over loving cheeks
    when choking grief decides to bite.
Those favourite places
    are now just empty spaces.
Reminders of another time
    when your heart slipped in mine.

DOWN IN CHINA TOWN

In the heart of the city
    where that beat can be found.
A vein of life
    pulses to that sound.
Lanterns bob in the early breeze
    teasing the stiffness of the naked trees.
They dance and sway in the murky grey
    forcing a smile to travel this way.

The sky cracks
    and the street is drenched.
But that bustle of life
    cannot be quenched.
Taste and smell banquet in the open air
    the chatter of life heard everywhere.
Stay and pay or take away
    but noone ever just walks away.

The street reflects
    as the pools meet the sky.
Lazy travellers miss this vision
    as cultures manage this great collision.
Tolerance and cooperation
    growing investments in this nation.
Where beauty hides in unlikely places
    in different tongues and different faces.

The Battle For Spring

White stallions ride down the winter storm
    their riders lost
        their bridles broken.
The sky falls into the depths of the sea
    waves boom and thunder
        as if their God has spoken.

Frothy images writhe in frustration
    boiling in their salty broth
        sulking in a reckless anger.
A blind rage claws for purchase
    calling the tide into battle
        an ever willing soldier.

A synthetic rock rises above the fury
    with time its only ally
        to defend this holy ground.
The fight continues with infinite rounds
    for the seconds are out
        and the bell makes no sound.

Spring jumps the ropes and enters the ring
    holds winter by the throat
        no longer strong and brave.
An audible hush covers the bay
    soothing the manic wrath
    as winter slips beneath the waves.

A FUNERAL BY ANY OTHER NAME

Winter casts the day in a granite stone
    a place where autumn
        is laid to rest.
Chiselled into a time of aching dread
    where the beat slowly fades
        and all colour is dead.

Black and white take the throne
    giving birth to a clan
        of unremarkable grey.
A shroud that drapes over every scene
    covering every trace
        where colour has been.

Tear drops fall from an emotional sky
    each tear a memory
        of a flourishing spring.
Now splashing on a concrete floor
    running down drains
        whenever it rains.

No homage is paid to this treacherous season
    naked trees stand in captivity
        refusing to bow or break.
Prisoners of a recurring defeat
    where the cavalry never comes
        and certainty takes the seat.

A ray of light breaks the horizon
    a warning shot across the bow
        cracks the arrogant gloom.
The ground splits as life climbs out
    gasping in the light
        to see the earth in bloom.

ABOUT THE AUTHOR

Alan lives in the holiday town of Ilfracombe with his wife Shula and dog Buster, a lovely place which looks over the Bristol Channel towards the island of Lundy. A few miles up the coast are the twin towns of Lynton and Lynmouth and the gateway to Exmoor.

Alan has 3 grown up children and 8 grandchildren, who also live in the town and another new arrival is imminent.

Alan grew up in the little village of Berrynarbor, between Combe Martin and Ilfracombe, after moving from London with his family in 1970 at the age of 9 and he still remembers the people that were part of those formative years that have made him much of who he is today. A very different experience from the hustle and bustle of the London suburbs.

Alan lost his Mum early and at the age of 13, he started to write, encouraged by Mr Crighton his English teacher. He told me to write about everything and anything, he called it "painting pictures in words" and over the years this is what I have tried to do, sometimes successfully and sometimes not.

Printed in Great Britain
by Amazon

26442452R00047